About the Author

Mark Vaughn has self-published many books of poetry and fiction through Amazon Books. He has worked as a minister and a physician's assistant, and has worked under the trade name 'Wordsmith' since 2004.

The Torch
The Annie Moore Story

Mark Vaughn

The Torch
The Annie Moore Story

Olympia Publishers
London

www.olympiapublishers.com
OLYMPIA PAPERBACK EDITION

Copyright © Mark Vaughn 2020

The right of Mark Vaughn to be identified as author of
this work has been asserted in accordance with sections 77 and 78
of the Copyright, Designs and Patents Act 1988.

All Rights Reserved

No reproduction, copy or transmission of this publication
may be made without written permission.
No paragraph of this publication may be reproduced,
copied or transmitted save with the written permission of the
publisher, or in accordance with the provisions
of the Copyright Act 1956 (as amended).

Any person who commits any unauthorised act in relation to
this publication may be liable to criminal
prosecution and civil claims for damage.

A CIP catalogue record for this title is
available from the British Library.

ISBN: 978-1-78830-610-2

This is a work of fiction.
Names, characters, places and incidents originate from the writer's
imagination. Any resemblance to actual persons, living or dead, is
purely coincidental.

First Published in 2020

Olympia Publishers
Tallis House
2 Tallis Street
London
EC4Y 0AB

Printed in Great Britain

Dedication

This book is dedicated to Emmitt Lamont Moore and his lovely wife, Ruth.

Acknowledgements

National Archives of the United States of America, and the Statue of Liberty foundation.

Drum-Taps by Walt Whitman

FIRST, O songs, for a prelude,
Lightly strike on the stretch'd tympanum, pride and joy in my city,
How she led the rest to arms – how she gave the cue,
How at once with lithe limbs, unwaiting a moment, she sprang;
(O superb! O Manhattan, my own, my peerless!
O strongest you in the hour of danger, in crisis! O truer than steel!)
How you sprang! how you threw off the costumes of peace with
indifferent hand;
How your soft opera-music changed, and the drum and fife were heard
in their stead;
How you led to the war, (that shall serve for our prelude, songs of
soldiers,)
How Manhattan drum-taps led.

Forty years had I in my city seen soldiers parading;

Forty years as a pageant – till unawares, the Lady of this teeming and
turbulent city,
Sleepless amid her ships, her houses, her incalculable wealth,
With her million children around her – suddenly,
At dead of night, at news from the south,
Incens'd, struck with clench'd hand the pavement.

A shock electric – the night sustain'd it;
Till with ominous hum, our hive at day-break pour'd out its myriads.

From the houses then, and the workshops, and through all the doorways,
Leapt they tumultuous – and lo! Manhattan arming.

To the drum-taps prompt,
The young men falling in and arming;
The mechanics arming, (the trowel, the jack-plane, the blacksmith's
hammer, tost aside with precipitation;)
The lawyer leaving his office, and arming – the judge leaving the
court;
The driver deserting his wagon in the street, jumping down, throwing
the reins abruptly down on the horses' backs;
The salesman leaving the store – the boss, book-keeper, porter, all leaving;
Squads gather everywhere by common consent, and arming;

The new recruits, even boys – the old men show them how to wear their accoutrements – they buckle the straps carefully;
Outdoors arming – indoors arming – the flash of the musket-barrels;
The white tents cluster in camps – the arm'd sentries around – the sunrise cannon, and again at sunset;
Arm'd regiments arrive every day, pass through the city, and embark from the wharves;
(How good they look, as they tramp down to the river, sweaty, with their guns on their shoulders!
How I love them! how I could hug them, with their brown faces, and their clothes and knapsacks cover'd with dust!)
The blood of the city up – arm'd! arm'd! the cry everywhere;
The flags flung out from the steeples of churches, and from all the public buildings and stores;
The tearful parting – the mother kisses her son — the son kisses his mother;
(Loth is the mother to part – yet not a word does she speak to detain him;)
The tumultuous escort – the ranks of policemen preceding, clearing the way;
The unpent enthusiasm – the wild cheers of the crowd for their favorites;
The artillery – the silent cannons, bright as gold, drawn along, rumble lightly over the stones;
(Silent cannons – soon to cease your silence!
Soon, unlimber'd, to begin the red business;)
All the mutter of preparation – all the determin'd arming;
The hospital service – the lint, bandages, and medicines;
The women volunteering for nurses – the work begun for, in earnest – no mere parade now;

War! an arm'd race is advancing! – the welcome for battle – no turning away;
War! be it weeks, months, or years – an arm'd race is advancing to welcome it.

Mannahatta a-march! – and it's O to sing it well!
It's O for a manly life in the camp!
And the sturdy artillery!
The guns, bright as gold – the work for giants – to serve well the guns:
Unlimber them! no more, as the past forty years, for salutes for courtesies merely;
Put in something else now besides powder and wadding.

And you, Lady of Ships! you Mannahatta!
Old matron of the city! this proud, friendly, turbulent city!
Often in peace and wealth you were pensive, or covertly frown'd amid all your children;
But now you smile with joy, exulting old Mannahatta!

Preface

The Annie Moore story is one that has become legend mixed with a little myth. Very likely, not even Annie Moore told her own story accurately together. What happened to Annie and her brothers is mostly found in vital records and statistics, and not even those are completely reliable.

The Torch mixes all the elements available with the myth, and the compelling question, why would a thirteen-year-old girl travel to the United States of America, and be the first to cross at Ellis Island? The New York Post recorded that she was fourteen, and had parents waiting for her in Queens. It was said that a colonel gave Annie a ten-dollar gold piece. She was said to have died in Texas, and is buried in Queens. There was an Annie Moore on record in Texas. There was also an Annie Moore Schayer buried in a Queens, New York cemetery. There was an Anne Moore of a Matthew and Julia Moore, born in Cork, and baptized in an infant baptism in 1874; much too soon for the thirteen-year-old who made the crossing. If born in 1874, she would have been eighteen, much different from the lady found on the ship's manifest and the one recorded as the first immigrant in the New York newspapers.

A song written in her honor much later describes her as a fifteen-year-old. In both Ireland and New York there are statues of Annie, and of Annie and her brothers.

So what is the real story? The ship's manifest states that Annie Moore thirteen, Anthony Moore eleven, and Phillip Moore were aboard the *SS Nevada* and made berth January 2, 1892. There were many such children who made their way to the land of opportunity in such a way. Annie was the second listed on the ship's manifest, her brothers third and fourth. Annie Schayer had eleven children.

The actual names of Annie's parents and her history from Ireland, is much like the other tales from lore. They are mixed with legend and embellished a bit, every family wanting to be related in some way to the girl who magically has inspired many with her adventure.

The Torch is an effort to examine those questions of Why and How, based on an honest examination of the history of the times. Although The Torch is historical fiction, it is not meant to embellish the story further, but add to the wonder of it. And in the same tradition as epic adventures such as Braveheart, and Michael Collins, it is an effort to capture the spirit of the statue that stands in New York harbor made by a Frenchman that has been an inspiration not only for Annie's time, but for all time.

Prologue

Helios clambered aboard his golden chariot for his daily ride across the sky. The Colossus Giant held his torch to give all the land light. Without the light, there would be nothing. The evening was lit by the lesser lights, cousins, hardly sufficient to carry the load that his simple ride every day could provide for all mankind.

The sky took on a purple glow and then broke into colors of red and pink, and, finally, Helios emerged in full stride at the beginning of a new day.

Chapter One
Manhattan Streets

It glowed its wealth on an island in New York harbor as well as on the horizon. As the sun peaked up from the waters of the Atlantic, all of New York came to life.

The city bustled with action. The dirt and cobbled stone roads were busy with horse and buggy and pedestrian traffic. Off in the distance was the sound of a foghorn as a boat announced its intentions in the harbor.

"Extra, Extra!" cried the voice of a boy with a stack of papers. The New York Post was at the top of the stack, and the headlines were in large black letterings. It read 'Brooklyn Bridge Announced'.

"I'll take one," said a handsome lady in a fine emerald green dress, with fancy lace and buttons. She had a handbag to match and a hat that had the appearance of being from Twelfth Avenue, where all the aristocratic and well-to-dos did their shopping. She reached into her bag and took out a small coin purse, pulled out a dime and handed it to the adolescent boy. He wore coveralls and a captain's hat.

"Here you are, ma'am," he said to her with a smile.

She reached into her purse again and pulled out a Morgan dollar. "Take this and get something special for your mother."

"Yes, ma'am," he said. He couldn't have been more than eleven years old. He didn't actually have a mother, at least one that he knew. He was one of the street urchins who was orphaned, living on the streets of Manhattan by whatever means they could.

It wasn't a question the benevolent lady asked when giving charity. It mattered not to her whether he spent it on his mother, someone else's mother, or himself. The important thing was that he had the Morgan dollar in his keep.

The woman's name was Emma Lazarus, daughter of Jewish immigrants from Portugal. Her parents were indeed well-to-do, or at least she wanted everyone to think so. Actually, she could relate to the street urchins, though never one actually herself. She really knew nothing of living on the streets but had endured a few hard times in her life, but today she was all smiles as the sunshine beamed down from a sun high in the sky hung like a giant torch. She had been writing a poem based on old Greek myths and decided a torch bearer of another kind might be best suited for her theme.

Her business today was a meeting with a poet, actually two poets, distinguished authors in their own right. One had taken a keen interest in her work, and her look, more so than the other distinguished authors and poets she kept in her stead.

She walked in a door and up some stairs and stopped at an upstairs apartment which had a balcony that overlooked Twelfth Street. She knocked on a rather worn wooden door which had once been painted white, or at least some form of off-white. An older gentleman opened the door after she knocked. She heard from behind the door a muffled acknowledgment and a promise that he would open it soon.

"Ah, Emma," said a man dressed in a blazer with a handkerchief, an eye-piece in one pocket, and a watch in the other.

"Hello, Waldo," she responded.

"Tea," said another voice at the coffee table, holding up a cup from a nearby saucer.

"You know Emma don't you, Robert?" smiled Waldo. He was Ralph Waldo to some, Mr. Emerson to others, and on his birth certificate was Ralph Waldo Emerson. Here he was just Waldo, and preferred it that way.

"Certainly," said Robert with a smile.

"Don't mind if I do, and an adieu to you," said Emma, rather playfully.

"So you enjoy a good joust, do you," asked Robert... he was Bob to some, but Robert, always, when in distinguished company such as he had today. It was his apartment in which Waldo was living with him. He was actually an unknown, an assistant, especially with a room available in New York city.

"I'd rather have tea," she said.

"We'll always have Paris," said Robert.

"I thought we were here to talk about the Pedestal... yes, yes, Pedestal poem."

Emma began to giggle a little after seeing Waldo a touch flustered by the moment. Emma didn't kiss and tell, but some of the poets did. And Waldo was quite impressed with her poetry... and her look. Unfortunately, Emma knew it.

"Tea, yes," said Waldo. He poured from a pot on a nearby stand into a cup there also and handed it to her. "Sugar?"

"Please," said Emma, and Waldo blushed; Robert laughed.

"Relax, Waldo, sit down," said Robert.

"The poem," said Emma.

Chapter Two
The Lady

It was dusk, and now the sun was setting. Waldo and Emma were on one of their regular strolls on the harbor front. Behind them were the tall buildings of the city, now draped in the scarlet of the ending day, and to their front, shipping. How majestic, at times, the industrial age could be. How wondrous the modern conveniences of the world as America approached the end of the nineteenth century. One of them with sails full, headed out to sea. Another closer by, had its stacks billowing out vast clouds of steam. The latter blew its horn.

"So, this is the poem you will be reading tomorrow night?" asked Emma, holding Waldo's arm as she walked closely, looking down seriously at a piece of parchment.

"Yes, yes," said Waldo. "How I do love the lights of the city. Will you be reading yours for the contest?"

"Certainly, wouldn't want the talents of good poet laureates to go to waste," said Emma with a smile, pulling Waldo close to her with his arm, snuggling up under his shoulder. This produced a slight laugh and a smile from Emerson.

"Do you want to practice?" asked Waldo.

Emma smiled. "Practice what?"

Waldo smiled. "The poem, silly."

"You first," she said.

'Twas the Night before Christmas

Twas the night before Christmas, when all thro' the house,
Not a creature was stirring, not even a mouse;

The stockings were hung by the chimney with care,
In hopes that St. Nicholas soon would be there;

The children were nestled all snug in their beds,
While visions of sugar plums danc'd in their heads,

And Mama in her 'kerchief, and I in my cap,
Had just settled our brains for a long winter's nap-

When out on the lawn there arose such a clatter,
I sprang from the bed to see what was the matter.

Away to the window I flew like a flash,
Tore open the shutters, and threw up the sash.

The moon on the breast of the new fallen snow,
Gave the lustre of mid-day to objects below;

When, what to my wondering eyes should appear,
But a miniature sleigh, and eight tiny rein-deer"

Emma gave him a bemused look.

With a little old driver, so lively and quick,
I knew in a moment it must be St. Nick.

"Did Robert assist you with that one?" asked Emma.
"Actually, he wrote it," said Waldo.
Emma laughed.
"Your turn," said Waldo.
Emma let loose of Waldo's arm and strode out to the edge of the pier on which they were now standing. She faced the horizon as if she had an audience, and certainly she had a view of the island named 'Liberty', soon to be the home of the Lady for who she wrote.

Not like the brazen giant of Greek fame
With conquering lights astride from land to land
Here at our sea washed, sunset gates shall stand
A mighty woman with a torch, whose flame
Is the imprisoned lightning, and her name…

She paused briefly, looking up. "Oh, what was her name?"
"Melba, I think," said Waldo.
Emma broke out into a laugh. "You're no help. Mother of Exiles."
"How could you forget a name like that," laughed Waldo, mimicking Robert from earlier in the day.
Emma blushed a little, hardly noticeable in the surrounding dusk.
"Let me start again," she said.

"Yes, yes…" said Waldo. "Get it right…"

She began again, keeping her composure with a smile that subtly faded as she continued with the poem.

From her beacon-hand
Glows a world-wide welcome, her mild eyes command
The air-bridged harbor that twin cities frame.
Keep ancient lands, your storied pomp.

She spoke with a louder voice as if she was trying to shout it to those on the Jersey shores.

"Give me your tired, your poor, your huddled masses, yearning to breathe free. The wretched refuse of your teeming shore. Send these, the homeless, the tempest tossed to me, I lift my lamp beside the golden door." As she finished, almost as if in answer… the sun ducked behind the city.

"All kidding aside, that one should be out on that pedestal," said Waldo.

Emma looked tentative, and then smiled. She walked over to Waldo and kissed his cheek.

Off in the distance, a lamp man finished his task of lighting the lanterns around the city. As she kissed him again, this time on his lips, if a person had been standing just right, it could be a rendering on canvas or a picture on a card.

He returned her affection and then took her by the arm again.

"I guess you will still go abroad?" asked Waldo.

"I don't know, Waldo," she said.

Waldo left by train the next day. Emma was to never hear from him again. A bit of a stubborn fellow with his constitutionals, he caught pneumonia one bitter evening. Emma found herself alone with her decision now

The meetings with the various committee members regarding the pedestal fund always led to the same thing. Raising money. Thomas Dewey had been a strong advocate. He had been one who was in favor of her traveling in Europe for just that reason. It was an exciting prospect. It was now up to her.

A church bell chimed close by. It was eight o'clock.

Emma Lazarus stood in her small bedroom and looked out the draped window. She had received word her friend Waldo had died. An article had been published in the Atlantic Monthly. Even she had admonished Waldo to take better care of himself. He had caught a cold walking in the rain. It developed into pneumonia. Mr. Longfellow had just perished as had David.

His friend Daniel had sculpted a bust. It was of Waldo and had been draped in a white robe. Waldo had endorsed Mr. French In the efforts to create a statue for the Minute Man. It had been just over one hundred years ago that the farmers and other townsmen had stood against the British regulars at the now famous bridge.

A may breeze blew the curtains.

Waldo had spoken of Europe in discussions and about the possibilities. Louisa May Alcott was at the funeral. She had idolized Waldo, as did she. She had traveled in Europe.

A walk at the harbor in the fresh air would help with the day's affairs. She heard the loud bellow of a boat's horn on the river. A walk down the street and a carriage ride brought her quickly to the harbor. It looked a bit different now. The Brooklyn Bridge was nearing its completion. The planners had stated that this year was the year. But next year was much more likely. Traveling abroad would something Waldo might smile about. She decided. She would go.

The boats on the river traveled to and fro. One passed by an island in the middle of the Hudson River. One day a Statue would be raised on the island.

She would write her acknowledgement and send it first thing. She would let them know she was going. One of the boat's horn sounded again in agreement.

The sun had not come up yet in San Francisco. There was an eight-year-old boy who was still asleep. His family would soon be moving east. A European adventure would possibly be in his future. His family was well to do. His name was Robert.

A man of some note, a transplant had already headed to east. His name was Samuel.

The sky in the east was becoming lighter with purples and reds. The morning stars were still brightly lit. Some who had known Presidents were now among them. Soon the sun would rise announcing with the dawn what was yet to come.

Chapter Three
Londonderry

The audience sat quietly as Emma Lazarus took to the platform. She missed Waldo. A rather quaint friend of quiet renown… She had not heard from him since she had left home. She hoped the letters would soon catch up with her. She loved the scenery, but the new culture took some getting accustomed to. She was helping to raise money for the Pedestal Fund. To place Bartholdi's statue upon the island erect, it needed a stable platform. On that platform would be her words. She had asked Waldo what it was like to gain national attention for a poem. He simply stared off into space and then, as if distracted, smiled and said…, "It's always an honor." She now understood the bittersweet silence before the answer. For one's words to gain the immortality of bronze lettering, it seemed the attention was the price at times. But the audiences were always nice to perform for. She was to recite a poem by Waldo. Perhaps that was the reason for the melancholy in her tone.

> By the nude bridge that arched the flood
> Their flag to April's breeze unfurled

Here once the embattled farmers stood.
And fired the shot heard 'round the world

The foe long since in silence slept
Alike the conqueror silent sleeps
And time the ruined bridge has swept
Down the dark stream which seaward creeps

On this green bank, by this soft stream
We set today a votive stone
That memory may their dead redeem
When like ourselves our sons are gone

Spirit, that made those heroes dare
To die, or leave their children free
Bid time and nature greatly spare
The shaft we raise to thee.

In the audience was a young lady with her mother. It was hard to tell her age, but she was pretty and spry; certainly she had the darting eyes of intelligence. Her mother was a fan of poetry. She listened intently to Emma as she spoke. "Those two poems are by two men who assisted me as I wrote this one. This one, as you know, was the Pedestal Fund winner," said Mrs. Lazarus. There was hearty applause, and the intense silence.

She began again, "Not like the brazen giant of Greek fame,

With conquering limbs astride from land to land;
Here at our sea-washed, sunset gates shall stand
A mighty woman with a torch, whose flame

> Is the imprisoned lightning, and her name
> Mother of Exiles. From her beacon-hand
> Glows world-wide welcome; her mild eyes command
> The air-bridged harbor that twin cities frame.

As she reached the climax of the evening, she spoke as if she were standing next to New York Harbor again.

> Keep ancient lands, your storied pomp!" cries she
> With silent lips. "Give me your tired, your poor,
> Your huddled masses yearning to breathe free,
> The wretched refuse of your teeming shore.
> Send these, the homeless, tempest-tost to me,
> I lift my lamp beside the golden door!

Chapter Four
Home

It had been a long trip for Uncle Wilbur. It was nice to see the farm in the distance. Samuel was his brother. Sam had married the village beauty, Elisabeth. Wilbur was a widower now finding family with Samuel and Elisabeth, but did from time to time visit a lady in Portugal. Wilbur had fled to Portugal when he first married, after words with his father. After his father had died, Wilbur returned.

"Well, Annie, what did you think?" asked Uncle Wilbur. They were riding in a carriage.

Annie nodded politely.

"The cat has your tongue, lass," he said with a smile.

Annie smiled shyly. Elisabeth looked over, Annie sitting between them.

"She didn't let us down, not at all," responded Elisabeth as she looked the other way out of the window at the passing landscape.

The Moores spoke in hushed whispers about America, and the poems had lifted all their spirits. The blight of the thirties had struck all in the village hard.

"Emma seemed rather sad about something," said Annie.

"She's a long way from home, lass," said Uncle Wilbur.

"Momma says that Ms. Lazarus is from Portugal," said Annie.

"Her family, darling," said Elisabeth.

"I may have met Ms. Lazarus' mother," said Uncle Wilbur.

There was a pause with just the rattle of the carriage and the rhythmic clap of the horses' trot.

There were doubting looks by both Annie and Elisabeth. "I may have."

"I may be dating her," said Uncle Wilbur. All three broke out into laughter.

One more bend in the road, a kind of blind turn, and they would be at their village. Wilbur had seen this turn many times before. He occasionally would teach in Lisbon at a university there. Up ahead, Annie's brother ran towards them as the carriage slowed. Samuel was standing on the corner, smiling.

"Welcome home," they heard Wilbur say. The carriage door opened, and all three emerged.

Chapter Five
The Eternal Flame

The dining table was ordinary, but the food was not. There were dishes full of vegetables and mutton, and breads that were exquisite. There was a rhubarb pie waiting patiently for the end of the meal, to be sliced. Samuel sat quietly sipping slowly at his beer as he listened to his brother tell his tales and entertain. All eyes were on Uncle Wilbur as he spoke.

"So, Lord Barton says to me, 'I think it's breech, what am I to do?' Samuel says, 'Well, pull the legs, damn you'." All laughed. "Well, he pulled on the horse's arse, and soon fell on his."

"Was the colt alright?" asked Philip with wide eyes.

"Oh yes, laddie." Even Samuel was smiling now. Elisabeth was enjoying herself. She loved it now that Wilbur was around. Samuel would take chances. Wilbur seemed to calm him.

"You promised the kids a story," said Elisabeth.

"Ah yes," said Wilbur. He looked to his brother. "What will it be tonight?" he asked. "Well, give the honor to the man of the house."

"How about the Greek Legend of the Great Colossus," said Samuel. "You tell it, Wilbur."

"Alright." said Wilbur. "That actually would be perfect with the reading of the New Colossus.

"They say that every morning, a great giant rises, early. His job, to carry the light across the sky after the moon goes to bed like the owls in the day. But with this giant, there would be no day. For the very torch he lights and carries is the light of the sun. He is big and strong like Atlas, but flies above the Earth. And his chariot golden. He lights his torch and then rides from the east to the west till he rests as the twilight brings on the night."

"What's his name, Uncle Wilbur?" asked Phillip. Quietly, Anthony and Annie looked on, listening intently.

"Helios is one name given," Wilbur said, and then he told how the Greeks would have games in his honor, taking a light from his torch to light their own until their games were finished. He was joined by a lady, but no one knew her name, always content as the games would bring him rest and satisfaction at a job well-done."

"The New Colossus is a lady," said Wilbur. "The Mother of Exiles."

All were hushed as the fire blazed and crackled in the fireplace.

"Perhaps, she was the lady," he finally said. Samuel pulled at his pipe, and Elisabeth smiled.

"Now bedtime," she said.

"A poem, Mother," said Annie. "Please."

"OK," she said, "But then time for bed."

I long for the sea

To find my destiny
Get me aboard a great ship
Let the westerlies prevail
For as I set my eyes
Upon the distant shore
I shall be happy
Evermore.

Again, there was hush. Not one word spoken about hopes for tomorrow. About hope for those distant shores.

"Now, off to bed," said Elisabeth.

Chapter Six
Troubles

"Anthony," said Samuel, "You're doing fine."

Anthony, eleven, seemed small behind the mule pulling the plow. He appeared to be holding on for dear life as he leaned back into it. He had plowed several rows. Phillip was chasing after Annie. Both were running toward Wilbur off in the distance.

"Let's get us some lunch," said Samuel. "Wilbur!"

Uncle Wilbur was on hands and knees planting potatoes. He stood.

They began to head towards the cottage for a quick bite. As they did, off in the distance, dust from the road began to make a gathering cloud as a carriage approached. The carriage stopped, seemingly blocking their way to the cottage, and two well-dressed businessmen stepped out.

"What can I do for you?" said Samuel, rather sternly.

"We understand you have a lease with a Mr. Barton," said the taller of the two gentlemen. The shorter of the two eyed Samuel intently as if studying for some weakness or flaw.

"That's Lord Barton," said Samuel. "Yes, I do."

"Come along, Annie," said Wilbur. He stood to the back of the carriage as he ushered the three children towards Elisabeth, now waiting anxiously at the door.

"I see," said the gentleman, and he said some quiet words with the shorter gentleman who wore a monocle.

The two men climbed back in their carriage.

"We'll be back to discuss this with you," the taller spokesman said as they suddenly departed.

"Will you be in that carriage?" asked Samuel with a bit more tact as if their departure had brought relief from some deep anxiety.

"Yes, of course," said the shorter gentleman.

"I'll be looking for you then," said Samuel.

Wilbur looked at Samuel, and then watched the carriage head down the road.

"Call the lads," said Samuel. Lunch had been interrupted.

Chapter Seven
The Bend

It was dusk. A squirrel skittered up a tree, seemingly oblivious to what was coming. The presence of the men was a concern, but nothing the squirrel had not seen before. It sat high above them, shouting insults for interrupting his afternoon to the six men at the pass.

The bend in the road was a treacherous spot. While it was in viewing distance of the farmland, it was several miles from Lord Barton's and the village. It was easy to conceal someone from the sight of oncoming traffic both ways. Samuel had the lads with him. There were two lookouts high on a hill about two miles further up the road. They could easily signal without revealing their position.

There were men in the village, the women and children taken to shelter at Lord Barton's estate. Lord Barton would be with them. He had once involved himself in the troubles but was much more trouble to Samuel than help. Samuel politely let him know he was far more valuable alive than being killed in this nasty business.

Samuel had never served in the military. But Samuel knew strategy taught to him in the troubles. He was captain of the guard, a kind of minuteman for his village, well respected by everyone. He knew the weight of what was occurring, and had seen the short one before. He was from Belfast. In a word, trouble.

Off in the distance, his scouts let them know of the number, they were on their way.

"There is a carriage, strong man on the top, and several on horses," said a man who had just arrived from forward. "Those two men." He smiled. "They were with them."

"Damn fools," said Samuel. "The dynamite set."

There were nods. The wires pulled the handle ready.

"As planned," said Samuel, then all disappeared, and the squirrel quieted. This he knew as well. There was nowhere to run and hide now.

All crouched down. They could hear the horses and the carriage. Samuel held the handle to the explosives.

"Wait," he thought.

The horses, tired from their journey, were beginning to blow a bit. All was quiet around the carriage as if they knew. Samuel could imagine the moves of his men forward as the ambush was now set. Samuel could sense them, almost see them. Sweat dripped off his forehead. The lad next to him looked expectant. The carriage had made the bend in the road.

Samuel pushed the handle.

The squirrel ran.

Chapter Eight
Sorrows

There was an explosion that deafened all the men that were present, those who survived the blast. A whole hillside seemingly fell onto the road, and the horses whinnied and scurried as riders or carriage men tried to rein then in. The men riding shotgun on the horses immediately began looking for targets. They soon had something to fire at.

A great cry erupted from the opposite side of the road, and gunfire echoed in the countryside. It was heard all the way to a horse barn where Uncle Wilbur was guarding Samuel's wife and children. He had a worried, but determined, look on his face. As Elisabeth and Annie and the two boys looked his way, his look softened. All eyes were wide with anxiety and anticipation. They could hear the yells and screams; then a familiar voice, but yelling angrily. It was Samuel hollering orders to his lads.

Elisabeth felt hot tears escaping from her eyes. Annie snuggled close to her mother, as her brother snuggled close to her. She was a little mother hen herself. But in this hour, there was no comfort to be felt, except in the shotgun that Uncle Wilbur held close, safety on.

Then there was quiet. Not even the animals made a noise. It was as if the world had stopped for a moment. Then sleep, except Wilbur. Exhaustion had finally taken its toll. Elisabeth reassured her children that soon they would be able to go home, but they would make the best of it here at Lord Barton's. Annie could teach the boys how to groom a horse, suggested Uncle Wilbur. Mrs. Barton opened the barn door with candle lit. Her face looked pale and gaunt, but she managed a smile as if to say, 'we'll be all right in a little bit, Samuel and his lads are out there'.

It seemed just a moment when sound of guns firing and explosions woke all in the barn again. This time, the anxiety was a bit fuller. Absolute fear had taken them. Wilbur's grip was tightened on his gun, and he rose to stand by the door in anticipation of an event he hoped would never occur. Then silence.

"Open the gate," came a voice. Samuel cracked the barn door. He slowly paused the barrel of the rifle outside. Then he recognized the rider.

"He's shot." Panic was written across his face. It was Samuel's best man. "We've got to find a doctor."

"Oh God," said Wilbur. "Oh God."

Samuel slid off the horse. He had been hit full in the chest. He was sucking in air, but was conscious. "Wilbur," he said. A tear fell... "Get Lizzy."

Soon, Lizzy and Annie and his boys were all by his side. Wilbur stood, hat off now, mumbling quiet prayers that mostly were heard as, 'Dear Jesus', and, 'Oh Mary, mother of God...'.

Finally, Wilbur was given a chance to speak to his dying brother.

"I'm sorry, Wilbur," Samuel said.

"Oh no," said Wilbur. "Oh, no… no worries, nothing to be sorrowful for… I love you, Samuel."

Sam smiled… then his eyes dilated and fixed, the smile strangely still remaining.

"Oh God," said Wilbur… and his tears fell freely.

Chapter Nine
Plans

Annie awoke to voices. It was Uncle Wilbur, he was talking to someone. She sat up and looked out of the barn door. She couldn't quite make out all the figures there in the morning sun.

"We can't go back, there's nothing there. I could take you with me to Lisbon, but it will take me a while to resettle."

Elisabeth nodded and mumbled something inaudible.

"You could go to Dublin," said a voice.

"I can check with my sister there, and see if we can stay in the back cottage for a while," said Elisabeth.

"That would give me time," said Uncle Wilbur.

His voice was very clear, not full of the grief heard last night. It was almost as if it was hiding mild embarrassment over the overwhelming show of emotion. Her momma's voice, however, still held the same grief, but very quietly as she spoke in hushed tones, with a voice she spent much effort to keep from breaking.

"Yes, we can't stay here. I agree with you."

The house, along with most of the village, was a complete loss. What they had brought with them was all that they had now. Annie had only known the cottage that now lay in ruin, as home. She wondered quietly what the future would bring. She was sure glad Wilbur was here.

"Annie?" said a quiet voce. It was Phillip.

"Come here, Phillip," she said. He snuggled close and she ran her fingers through his hair as her mother would hers from time to time, to comfort her. Anthony was awake, but was quietly dealing with the loss by rolling over and facing the barn opposite to the open door. Occasionally, a soft sob could be heard.

Chapter Ten
Another Goodbye

"Your mother," said Uncle Wilbur. His voice broke. He turned away. He told the priest he wanted to try to tell the children himself. The priest discouraged it because of the scene that occurred, but saw the need for it as well. He immediately took over as Wilbur collected himself, sitting on a nearby pew.

The children were completely attentive now as the catholic priest spoke.

"Your mother was shot and killed," he said. "I'm sorry."

The children were stunned; all had bunched up, leaning on Annie. Annie was mum now.

"Will Uncle Wilbur be alright?" was what Annie finally mustered herself to say. The words came out firmer than she expected. A strange strength was inside.

"Yes;" the priest answered and smiled, seeing it immediately in her eyes. This was a special child. He was certain God's protection would be with her and her brothers.

"Your uncle is seeking out some place safe for you to go. He said he thinks America might be the best possibility," said the priest.

Suddenly, both boys sat up a bit straighter.

"America," Phillip finally said.

"Wilbur has lived in Lisbon, and thinks maybe you would be able to find relatives in Queens. He hasn't heard from them, and getting in touch seems a challenge," the priest said. "You can stay here tonight."

Almost on cue, a nun walked out with some blankets and a warm smile.

"I'll be alright," said Wilbur as he stood. "Can we bury her here, Father?"

"Yes, son," he said, "We'll make arrangements."

Chapter Eleven
Sanctuary

How I long for green fields
The fields on which I ran
When I was young
And my world free of trouble
And with each sunrise
Each gull cries
Where even fig trees can grow
And in the morning
I could drink the dew
It seems from my nest
Are taken precious things
As robbers rob the peace I seek
I long to sing with the birds
And walk roads that lead
To places of the heart
And places of inner peace
What I long for most is
Sanctuary – **Elisabeth Moore**

Annie Moore was kneeling before a statue of the Mother Mary with her hands folded, eyes gazing upward. The statue of Mary had her arms spread as if in blessing. That is what Annie was praying for now. They could use all the help they could. Her Uncle Wilbur had returned briefly and gave her a journal with her mother's writings in them. It was mostly poetry and a few comments about life, and family. As she read, she learned how her mother loved American literature. She dreamed of reading poetry in New York on the stage. She always had wanted to learn to dance. But time had passed her by, perhaps with her poetry she could afford dance lessons for Annie, and music lessons for the boys.

"Annie," said Phillip, holding his brother's hand, "I have to go."

"What?" said Annie. Then she saw Phillip holding his legs together. "Oh," she laughed. Anthony laughed as well. He was quieter than usual, but a tremendous support in looking after Phillip. Both could tend to themselves, Anthony more independent than Phillip. But Phillip was only seven years old. Annie led Phillip outside. There was a small facility building near the inner garden at the outside wall. She led him there and waited. There was a bed pan for emergencies during the night but in the day, Annie would always escort the boys for her own comfort and theirs also.

"Uncle Wilbur will be here soon," said Annie as all were finished, and they returned into the sanctuary building. They rested near the back, out of the way of those who might arrive for services or prayer.

Soon, they heard Wilbur's voice.

"I have some sandwiches," said Uncle Wilbur. "The drink will burn a little when you swallow it. I want you to drink a little. It will keep you from dysentery."

They all walked out into the garden to eat. It was cold tonight with the rain. It was good to have a warm place to rest.

"I've found a way on a boat to New York," said Uncle Wilbur after taking a few bites. "We will make passage in the morning to the harbor."

The young faces all took this in; they twisted their lips as they drank the warm fluid.

Soon, they had finished their meal and all went to settle to rest and ready for the trip in the morning. Uncle Wilbur would sleep there tonight.

"America," said Annie as she tucked in her brothers. They both smiled nervous smiles. "Mother always wanted to go to America."

"So did Father," said Anthony.

"Yes," said Annie, the hurt still close, "Yes he did."

Uncle Wilbur sat on a bench near them, as if on watch. And soon all four were asleep.

A nun came by and covered Wilbur, and then put out all the lights, except one. Then she quietly left for her own bed.

In the stillness, all that could be heard then was the breathing of its resting occupants, and occasional mumblings from Wilbur as he battled some unseen foe.

Chapter Twelve
Flight

"Annie?" Annie heard a voice. It was Uncle Wilbur. A priest was with him. Also with them was the priest who had taken them in, and the nun who took care of them last night.

Annie woke her brothers, who were already stirring.

"This is Father Thomas," said the priest to all. "He will be taking you this morning."

"Hi, Annie," said Father Thomas. "I knew your mother when she was your age." He was graying, with a rather gray beard that was mottled at the edges.

Annie smiled. Her brothers were wide-eyed with anticipation.

"Not to worry, put on these," he said, handing them some prayer robes. He had also baptized Annie when she was born near the harbor where they would be heading to. Her mother was from near there. "Gather your things and we'll be off."

All of them then followed Father Thomas out of the church gates, and out into the streets. They were all dressed in the prayer robes and shawls as if they were monks. They walked right out into fields, and disappeared down a path next to a brook. The air was quite cool that morning, but none complained. Their breath could be seen down by the water. Soon, they found themselves at a barn with its door standing open. Inside was a wagon, and a man greeted them as they arrived.

"Wool coats," he said, as Annie and her brothers took off their prayer robes. Uncle Wilbur kept his. They all took a place on the wagon, which was ready to go. They heard someone say 'Godspeed' and they started up the road in the opposite direction, backtracking over the ground they had covered. Father Thomas stood at the door to the barn, smiling as he watched them go. After a bit, they were out of town and on country back roads headed for Cork.

They arrived at a small church briefly for breakfast. A nun named Mother Francis served them, along with a parishioner from a small Catholic monastery called St. Jonathan's Cathedral. Mother Superior led them inside and they rested, waiting on another wagon which would take them the rest of the way.

"Will you read to us, Uncle Wilbur?" asked Phillip as they all sat. They would rest here for the night.

"Sure," said Uncle Wilbur.

"This poem is called 1492; it is another one by Ms. Lazarus," said Uncle Wilbur. Annie smiled. All listened.

> Thou two-faced year, Mother of Change and Fate,
> Didst weep when Spain cast forth with flaming sword,
> The children of the prophets of the Lord,
> Prince, priest, and people, spurned by zealot hate.
> Hounded from sea to sea, from state to state,
> The West refused them, and the East abhorred.

No anchorage the known world could afford,
Close-locked was every port, barred every gate.
Then smiling, thou unveil'dst, O two-faced year,
A virgin world where doors of sunset part,
Saying, "Ho, all who weary, enter here!
There falls each ancient barrier that the art
Of race or creed or rank devised, to rear
Grim bulwarked hatred between heart and heart!

"What does it mean, Uncle Wilbur?" asked Anthony.

"That the New World gives us a place to go," said Uncle Wilbur, matter-of-factly.

It was quiet as all sat in their own thoughts, tired from the day's events. Then Phillip spoke up. "Will we ride in a steam ship?"

"The Nevada has sails as I understand it. But it will do just fine, lad," said Uncle Wilbur.

Chapter Thirteen
The Cliffs of Andover

Long Island Sound… by Emma Lazarus

    I see it as it looked one afternoon
    In August – by a fresh soft breeze o'erblown
    The swiftness of the tide, the light thereon.
    A far-off sail, white as a crescent moon.
    The shining waters with pale currents strewn,
    The quiet fishing-smacks, the Eastern cove,
    The semi-circle of its dark, green grove.
    The luminous grasses, the merry sun
    In the grave sky; the sparkle far and wide
    Laughter of unseen children, cheerful chirp
    Of crickets, and low lisp of rippling tide
    Light summer clouds fantastical as sleep
    Changing unnoted while I gazed thereon
    All these fair sounds and sights I made my own.

The travelers were near the ocean. At times, they had glimpses of sheer cliffs falling into the sea. As they topped one ridge, they could see the masts of the harbor. They felt the breath of wind on their faces from the ocean and smelled the fresh salt air. All were taken by the many sights.

It was not long till their wagon pulled alongside of a rather weather worn vessel, somewhat smaller than many of the others but seaworthy.

They did not have many bags, and unloaded what they had. Wilbur had gathered what he could as they made their way. They would be saying their goodbyes soon. All three had grown fonder of Wilbur over the last several days and weeks. They couldn't imagine him not being by their side.

A doctor looked them over before they boarded. Briefly, Wilbur spoke with the captain with whom he had made arrangements.

"Aye, I'll be along. You'll see after them?" asked Wilbur, handing the captain a coin.

"Aye," he said, taking the coin and placing it in a money purse. "I'll watch over them. I'll make sure they make it to Ellis Island. I'll wait till it is opened, it will be opening soon."

Soon, their dunnage was aft, and they were in a small dank cabin. Uncle Wilbur sat with them.

"Can you stay, Uncle Wilbur, till we leave?" asked Annie, the thoughts of the coming voyage clouding her eyes with unseen worries.

"Ah, my little lassie," said Uncle Wilbur. "You are so grown up," he said. His voice caught. "You'll do fine, lass, just fine."

Chapter Fourteen
Open Sea

Annie and her brothers were aloft for the departure of the Nevada. They leaned on the rails and watched with fascination as the ship's crew made preparations for departure. The tug gave them a push, and soon they were out of the harbor. The sails caught hold, the ship leaned into it, and soon the wind was on their face.

"Avast, ladies," shouted the captain, "And put your shoulder to it."

"She is hard to port," they heard the answer.

"Hold her steady," said the captain. "You there, down with that sail. Keep the rudder steady."

They looked as they kept a parallel course to the shore and then, as slowly, all that they had known became smaller and smaller. Then they went below. It would be a long journey. Immediately, sea sickness took its toll. They returned topside. Annie had a tougher time than her brothers it seemed, but later her brothers would say they had a tougher time with it than she.

The days and nights mixed together, with quick meals as they gained their sea legs, and restless sleep. One rain squall had them huddled in the corner saying their prayers. But then the quiet after seemed to never end, as they waited for wind to fill the Nevada's sails. As far as they could see was ocean blue. An occasional sea bird would remind them that somewhere was dry land.

Annie was lying down with her brothers when the captain came by.

"Getting your sea legs, lassie?" he asked in a gruff but friendly tone. A Hispanic woman down the way would check on them as well. She did not know English, and Annie did not know any Spanish, so they did the best they could with French. She was sitting with them. Everyone in the room seemed washed out by the journey, except the captain, who seemed invigorated by the journey.

"Your Uncle Wilbur asked me to give you this when we were getting close to shore," said the captain. It was a small envelope. He smiled and tipped his cap, and then excused himself. Annie opened it. It had instructions and some small bills – 'in case of emergency' it said. She would keep it close. She looked at the Spanish lady and she smiled.

Very soon they would see the shore of America.

Chapter Fifteen
New York Harbor

City Visions
by Emma Lazarus

I

As the blind Milton's memory of light,
The deaf Beethoven's phantasy of tone,
Wroght joys for them surpassing all things known
In our restricted sphere of sound and sight –
So while the glaring streets of brick and stone
Vix with heat, noise, and dust from morn till night,
I will give rein to Fancy, taking flight
From dismal now and here, and dwell alone
With new-enfranchised senses. All day long,
Think ye 't is I, who sit 'twixt darkened walls,
While ye chase beauty over land and sea?
Uplift on wings of some rare poet's song
Where the wide billow laughs and leaps and falls,
I soar cloud-high, free as the winds are free.

II

Who grasps the substance? who 'mid shadows strays?
He who within some dark-bright wood reclines,
'Twixt sleep and waking, where the needled pines
Have cushioned al his couch with soft brown sprays?
He notes not how the living water shines,
Trembling along the cliff, a flickering haze,
Brimming a wine-bright pool, nor lifts his gaze
To read the ancient wonders and the signs.
Does he possess the actual, or do I,
Who paint on air more than his sense receives,
The glittering pine-tufts with closed eyes behold,
Breathe the strong resinous perfume, see the sky
Quiver like azure flame between the leaves,
And open unseen gates with key of gold?

The cry of, "Land Ho," was a welcome one. Now, as they had watched their homeland disappear behind them, they watched as the shore became broader and more defined as they drew closer. It seemed that they would never arrive, then they saw their destination. The captain guided his ship towards a building, seemingly floating like a boat in the middle of New York harbor. On both shores were buildings large and small, and roadways filled with horses, carriages and people.

Next to their berth was a statue of a lady on another island. The lady of the poem they heard so long ago. Was it just last year? The lady held a torch. Annie remembered the words. She and her brothers were in need of her comfort, this Mother of Exiles. Certainly they missed theirs, and their dad.

They were on their own now, here. This was America. Somehow she dreamed of it differently. It seemed so harsh and coarse, so ordinary now. But the lady with the torch held the magic. Indeed, she would guide them with her light.

The captain came by again, letting them know of their schedule while in port and of their departure from the ship. In the morning, they would unload and enter into the building on the island for naturalization. But for now, rest.

It was strange not to be in motion. The ship rocked slowly as gulls flew by overhead. The distant sounds of the city replaced the sounds of the journey.

Chapter Sixteen
The Picture

"I want you to look like you just got off the boat. Everyone look natural." A photographer with his head under a curtain, kept popping his head out to get the picture correctly. This one was for posterity.

Finally, a disgruntled passenger muttered under his breath, "We did just get off the boat, mister."

There was mild laughter. The flash went off. A picture with kids mostly, standing in line at the doors of Ellis Island, was the result.

"Have time for one more?" he said.

"We're not going anywhere," said one of the kids in the crowd.

There was a bustle inside the building. This was their first day. It was its grand opening. People were in place, and the boats continued to pour passengers under the eaves just outside the main doors.

Pop went the camera bulb. Picture number two.

"None of you are Indian?" said the photographer. He was met with blank stares. "I just didn't want anyone mad at me for taking their spirit."

"So this is America," thought Annie. It wasn't that she didn't like the man taking the pictures, it was just... well.

"I mean there are some Injuns that stopped an engine out west somewhere. Don't like the iron horse."

Annie was somewhat familiar with bigotry, but not quite like this. Little did she know what awaited her once she crossed the harbor into Manhattan. The first amendment would allow for this, certainly the pursuit of happiness might counter, at least she hoped so. Maybe the life and liberty thing. There were parts of New York in which an Irish woman was looked upon like Injuns were looked upon.

Annie began wondering about the Indians. She sure would like to see an Indian. An iron horse? She had just ridden on a sail boat to Ellis Island.

Pop... another still picture. She wondered if she was smiling.

Ahead, the doors opened.

So this was America.

Pop, the bulb went off; the line was moving, she wondered if it messed up the man's picture.

So began Annie and her brothers' American Experience.

Chapter Seventeen
Ellis Island Madness

Everyone in the line was ushered into a large hallway, then into a great room. Annie and her brothers were right towards the front.

"Let me do the talking," said Annie to her brothers. All three were nervous. There was talk of sending some back home if they didn't achieve certain standards. They were healthy when they had left Cork, but the passage had left them weary worn. Even a sniffle, some said, might keep you out.

Annie was not at all worried about Phillip. She was worried about what Anthony might say. But usually he was quiet, especially in situations like this.

"Your name?" asked a lady at a counter. She had reading glasses.

"Annie Moore," said Annie. "These are my brothers, Phillip and Anthony. We need to stay together."

"What nationality?" she asked next.

"We're from Ireland," said Anthony. Annie cut her eyes at him.

"Irish, huh?" said the lady. "To the first door to the right for you doctor's examination."

Annie took her brothers' hands and did as she was told.

The doctor quickly took appraisal of them one by one. Annie managed to keep hold of her brothers as they dragged their things, room station to room station. A stamp here, a signature there.

"Age?" said a man.

"Fifteen," said Annie.

"Nuh-uh," said Phillip.

"Okay, fourteen." Annie shot a look of exasperation at her younger brother, who quickly clammed up.

"Your mother and father are in Queens?"

"Yes," said Annie. Her brothers stood with their mouths shut, expressionless. Annie had no idea where Wilbur was, he was the closest thing they had to kin right now. She had some names on a page to find in Queens right now, they were her mom and dad.

"Do you have their names?" said the man.

"Matthew and Julia Moore," said Annie, "Here on this document."

She quickly flashed on the counter a baptismal certificate of an infant baptism in Cork she had received in her packet from the captain. They had spent their waking hours in port reviewing what to do when they were asked certain questions.

"I am looking… for them," said the Spanish woman from their berth on the ship.

"They are your children?" he asked.

The woman was flustered by the question. "No."

"She is our nanny," said Annie.

"Very well," said the man. A few stamps on a document and they moved on.

Somewhere along the way, they became citizens of the United States of America.

"Welcome to the United States of America," said a younger gentleman as he led them to a barge. Their nanny was still behind one of the counters, she smiled and waved as they walked to the landing.

"Do you need help with your things?" he asked.

"Thank you," said Annie. She smiled, she thought he was handsome. He seemed oblivious to this, but he smiled a friendly smile anyway.

They stepped on to the ferry. This was their new home.

Welcome to America.

Chapter Eighteen
The Colonel

It was strange to be the only ones on the large ferry. The ferry captain said it was because they were the very first to receive their citizenship at Ellis Island. It had been a grueling process.

The captain came by to see them off. He would be leaving for Ireland soon. He asked them if they wanted to come along. Annie almost said yes, but Uncle Wilbur would be disappointed. It would get better. After all, this was America.

The ferry pulled away from the dock. They slowly crossed towards Battery Island where she would walk ashore with her brothers.

The building structures loomed. The waterway was full of bustle. But what captured Annie's attention was the lady high above them holding her torch: the mother of exiles.

The ride was actually quite quick for a ferry ride. They were ushered off the boat and the attendant gathered their things.

"A carriage, madam?" he asked.

She saw the young captain wave. She smiled and waved back.

"No thanks," she said.

A man walked up with a top hat.

"This lady is the first United States citizen from Ellis Island." He smiled and shook her hand. Then he kissed the back of her hand like she was royalty.

"And your name?" she heard someone yell.

"It is here on the manifest, she is Annie Moore of Ireland. Her mother and father are in Queens waiting for her and her brothers, Phillip and Anthony."

"How old is she?"

"Says here, fourteen," said the colonel. He was part of the greeting committee. There was no dispute from the three children, who looked as if they had washed up on shore after their experience.

"Here you are, lassie," he said to her. He handed her a ten-dollar gold piece. "This should get you started. Handsome!"

He looked back to Annie and her brothers. "To Queens?"

"Yes, please," managed Annie. She and her brothers hopped aboard.

"Do you need a guide, Annie?" asked the colonel.

"We'll manage," she said in her best adult voice. She certainly didn't feel the confidence she showed. But this was better than Ulster.

The carriage departed, kicking up cobble stones. They were in Manhattan, New York.

Chapter Nineteen
Two Years Later

Annie Moore did not feel sixteen, but she was. She actually felt older. She had come to Manhattan with Uncle Wilbur to see the Statue and Ellis Island from the landing.

It was dusk. As she looked out, the setting sun cast reds and purples across the harbor. The Brooklyn Bridge was being lit. She held in her hand her mother's journal. She read aloud from its pages.

"Do you think she can hear me?" she asked Wilbur.

"Certainly, and Samuel as well." The years had been hard on Wilbur, who had grayed a bit more. His shoulders sagged a little as he stood.

"I wonder if they would have liked America," Annie said aloud to herself.

"Do you like it?" asked Uncle Wilbur.

"Yes," said Annie. "Oh yes."

Uncle Wilbur smiled and took her hand on his arm.

He paid a young boy for his last newspaper.

"Thanks, mister," he said and scuttled off into the city streets.

Wilbur called for a carriage.
Yes indeed, it was America, the land of dreams.

from **Dreams,**
by Emma Lazarus

A dream of lilies all the blooming earth;
A garden full of fairies and of flowers
It's only music the glad cry of mirth
While the warm sun weaves golden-tissued hours,
Hope a bright angel,
beautiful
...true...

ISLE OF HOPE, ISLE OF TEARS
(Brendan Graham) Sean Keane
Also recorded by: Andy Cooney; Dolores Keane; Anthony Kearns; Ronan Tynan; Celtic Woman; Celtic Thunder.

On the first day of January,
Eighteen ninety-two,
They opened Ellis Island and they let
The people through.
And the first to cross the threshold
Of that isle of hope and tears,
Was Annie Moore from Ireland
Who was all of fifteen years.

CHORUS:
Isle of hope, isle of tears,

Isle of freedom, isle of fears,
But it's not the isle you left behind.
That isle of hunger, isle of pain,
Isle you'll never see again
But the isle of home is always on your mind.

In a little bag she carried
All her past and history,
And her dreams for the future
In the land of liberty.
And courage is the passport
When your old world disappears
But there's no future in the past
When you're fifteen years

CHORUS:
Isle of hope, isle of tears,
Isle of freedom, isle of fears,
But it's not the isle you left behind.
That isle of hunger, isle of pain,
Isle you'll never see again
But the isle of home is always on your mind.

When they closed down Ellis Island
In nineteen forty-three,
Seventeen million people
Had come there for sanctuary.
And in Springtime when I came here
And I stepped onto its piers,
I thought of how it must have been
When you're fifteen years.

CHORUS:

Isle of hope, isle of tears,
Isle of freedom, isle of fears,
But it's not the isle you left behind.
That isle of hunger, isle of pain,
Isle you'll never see again
But the isle of home is always on your mind.

Epilogue

Annie Moore moved to Queens, married and had eleven children. She was buried in Queens, New York, as Annie Schayer. There are countless named Moore who can trace their legacy at Ellis Island, at the Ellis Island memorial.

Annie and her brothers were the first of millions to pass through Ellis Island. Their legacy is still felt today.

Emma Lazarus' words and poems echoed the themes of many of her mentors, including Robert Frost and Ralf Waldo Emerson. From their poetry and that of their contemporaries, we have celebrated Christmas, ''Twas the Night Before Christmas'; studied psychology, 'The Road Less Traveled', and celebrated America in many, many poems.

Of Emma Lazarus' many poems, only one is well remembered. It is emblazoned in raised bronzed lettering on the Pedestal of the Statue of Liberty.

> Not like the brazen giant of Greek fame,
> With conquering limbs astride from land to land;
> Here at our sea-washed, sunset gates shall stand
> A mighty woman with a torch, whose flame
> Is the imprisoned lightning, and her name

Mother of Exiles. From her beacon-hand
Glows world-wide welcome; her mild eyes command
The air-bridged harbor that twin cities frame.
"Keep, ancient lands, your storied pomp!" cries she
With silent lips. "Give me your tired, your poor,
Your huddled masses yearning to breathe free,
The wretched refuse of your teeming shore.
Send these, the homeless, tempest-tost to me,
I lift my lamp beside the golden door!"
The New Colossus
Emma Lazarus, Pedestal Fund Contest Winner

Selected Poems of Emma Lazarus
Dreams

A DREAM of lilies: all the blooming earth,
A garden full of fairies and of flowers;
Its only music the glad cry of mirth,
While the warm sun weaves golden-tissued hours;
Hope a bright angel, beautiful and true
As Truth herself, and life a lovely toy,
Which ne'er will weary us, ne'er break, a new
Eternal source of pleasure and of joy.
A dream of roses: vision of Loves tree,
Of beauty and of madness, and as bright
As naught on earth save only dreams can be,
Made fair and odorous with flower and light;
A dream that Love is strong to outlast Time,
That hearts are stronger than forgetfulness,
The slippery sand than changeful waves that climb,
The wind-blown foam than mighty waters' stress.

A dream of laurels: after much is gone,
Much buried, much lamented, much forgot,
With what remains to do and what is done,
With what yet is, and what, alas! is not,
Man dreams a dream of laurel and of bays,
A dream of crowns and guerdons and rewards,
Wherein sounds sweet the hollow voice of praise,
And bright appears the wreath that it awards.
A dream of poppies, sad and true as Truth,–
That all these dreams were dreams of vanity;
And full of bitter penitence and ruth,
In his last dream, man deems 'twere good to die;
And weeping o'er the visions vain of yore,
In the sad vigils he doth nightly keep,
He dreams it may be good to dream no more,
And life has nothing like Death's dreamless sleep.

Long Island Sound
by Emma Lazarus
http://www.poemhunter.com/poem/long-island-sound/

I see it as it looked one afternoon
In August, by a fresh soft breeze o'erblown.
The swiftness of the tide, the light thereon,
A far-off sail, white as a crescent moon.
The shining waters with pale currents strewn,
The quiet fishing-smacks, the Eastern cove,
The semi-circle of its dark, green grove.
The luminous grasses, and the merry sun
In the grave sky; the sparkle far and wide,
Laughter of unseen children, cheerful chirp

Of crickets, and low lisp of rippling tide,
Light summer clouds fantastical as sleep
Changing unnoted while I gazed thereon.
All these fair sounds and sights I made my own.

1492
by Emma Lazarus

Thou two-faced year, Mother of Change and Fate,
Didst weep when Spain cast forth with flaming sword,
The children of the prophets of the Lord,
Prince, priest, and people, spurned by zealot hate.
Hounded from sea to sea, from state to state,
The West refused them, and the East abhorred.
No anchorage the known world could afford,
Close-locked was every port, barred every gate.
Then smiling, thou unveil'dst, O two-faced year,
A virgin world where doors of sunset part,
Saying, "Ho, all who weary, enter here!
There falls each ancient barrier that the art
Of race or creed or rank devised, to rear
Grim bulwarked hatred between heart and heart!"

City Visions
by Emma Lazarus

I

As the blind Milton's memory of light,
The deaf Beethoven's phantasy of tone,
Wroght joys for them surpassing all things known

In our restricted sphere of sound and sight –
So while the glaring streets of brick and stone
Vix with heat, noise, and dust from morn till night,
I will give rein to Fancy, taking flight
From dismal now and here, and dwell alone
With new-enfranchised senses. All day long,
Think ye 't is I, who sit 'twixt darkened walls,
While ye chase beauty over land and sea?
Uplift on wings of some rare poet's song
Where the wide billow laughs and leaps and falls,
I soar cloud-high, free as the winds are free.

II

Who grasps the substance? who 'mid shadows strays?
He who within some dark-bright wood reclines,
'Twixt sleep and waking, where the needled pines
Have cushioned all his couch with soft brown sprays?
He notes not how the living water shines,
Trembling along the cliff, a flickering haze,
Brimming a wine-bright pool, nor lifts his gaze
To read the ancient wonders and the signs.
Does he possess the actual, or do I,
Who paint on air more than his sense receives,
The glittering pine-tufts with closed eyes behold,
Breathe the strong resinous perfume, see the sky
Quiver like azure flame between the leaves,
And open unseen gates with key of gold?

Poems attributed to Elisabeth Moore in the text (by Mark Vaughn)

Evermore

I long for the sea
To find my destiny
Get me aboard a great ship
Let the westerlies prevail
For as I set my eyes
Upon the distant shore
I shall be happy
Evermore

Sanctuary

How I long for green fields
The fields on which I ran
When I was young
And my world free of trouble
And with each sunrise
Each Gull crys
Where even fig trees can grow
And in the morning
I could drink the dew
It seems from my nest
Are taken precious things
As robbers rob the peace I seek
I long to sing with the birds
And walk roads that lead
To places of the heart

And places of inner peace
What I long for most is
Sanctuary

Selected Poetry of Nineteenth and Twentieth Century American Poets

The Landlord's Tale. The Midnight Ride of Paul Revere's Ride
by Henry Wadsworth Longfellow

Listen, my children, and you shall hear
Of the midnight ride of Paul Revere,
On the eighteenth of April, in Seventy-five;
Hardly a man is now alive
Who remembers that famous day and year.

He said to his friend, "If the British march
By land or sea from the town to-night,
Hang a lantern aloft in the belfry arch
Of the North Church tower as a signal light,–
One, if by land, and two, if by sea;
And I on the opposite shore will be,
Ready to ride and spread the alarm
Through every Middlesex village and farm,
For the country folk to be up and to arm."
Then he said, "Good night!" and with muffled oar
Silently rowed to the Charlestown shore,
Just as the moon rose over the bay,
Where swinging wide at her moorings lay
The Somerset, British man-of-war;

A phantom ship, with each mast and spar
Across the moon like a prison bar,
And a huge black hulk, that was magnified
By its own reflection in the tide.

Meanwhile, his friend, through alley and street,
Wanders and watches with eager ears,
Till in the silence around him he hears
The muster of men at the barrack door,
The sound of arms, and the tramp of feet,
And the measured tread of the grenadiers,
Marching down to their boats on the shore.

Then he climbed the tower of the Old North Church,
By the wooden stairs, with stealthy tread,
To the belfry-chamber overhead,
And startled the pigeons from their perch
On the sombre rafters, that round him made
Masses and moving shapes of shade –
By the trembling ladder, steep and tall,
To the highest window in the wall,
Where he paused to listen and look down
A moment on the roofs of the town,
And the moonlight flowing over all.
Beneath, in the churchyard, lay the dead,
In their night-encampment on the hill,
Wrapped in silence so deep and still
That he could hear, like a sentinel's tread,
The watchful night-wind, as it went
Creeping along from tent to tent,
And seeming to whisper, "All is well!"

A moment only he feels the spell
Of the place and the hour, and the secret dread
Of the lonely belfry and the dead;
For suddenly all his thoughts are bent
On a shadowy something far away,
Where the river widens to meet the bay —
A line of black that bends and floats
On the rising tide, like a bridge of boats.

Meanwhile, impatient to mount and ride,
Booted and spurred, with a heavy stride
On the opposite shore walked Paul Revere.
Now he patted his horse's side,
Now gazed at the landscape far and near,
Then, impetuous, stamped the earth,
And turned and tightened his saddle girth;
But mostly he watched with eager search
The belfry-tower of the Old North Church,
As it rose above the graves on the hill,
Lonely and spectral and sombre and still.
And lo! as he looks, on the belfry's height
A glimmer, and then a gleam of light!
He springs to the saddle, the bridle he turns,
But lingers and gazes, till full on his sight
A second lamp in the belfry burns!
A hurry of hoofs in a village street,
A shape in the moonlight, a bulk in the dark,
And beneath, from the pebbles, in passing, a spark
Struck out by a steed flying fearless and fleet:
That was all! And yet, through the gloom and the light,
The fate of a nation was riding that night;

And the spark struck out by that steed, in his flight,
Kindled the land into flame with its heat.
He has left the village and mounted the steep,
And beneath him, tranquil and broad and deep,
Is the Mystic, meeting the ocean tides;
And under the alders, that skirt its edge,
Now soft on the sand, now loud on the ledge,
Is heard the tramp of his steed as he rides.

It was twelve by the village clock,
When he crossed the bridge into Medford town.
He heard the crowing of the cock,
And the barking of the farmer's dog,
And felt the damp of the river fog,
That rises after the sun goes down.

It was one by the village clock,
When he galloped into Lexington.
He saw the gilded weathercock
Swim in the moonlight as he passed,
And the meeting-house windows, blank and bare,
Gaze at him with a spectral glare,
As if they already stood aghast
At the bloody work they would look upon.

It was two by the village clock,
When he came to the bridge in Concord town.
He heard the bleating of the flock,
And the twitter of birds among the trees,
And felt the breath of the morning breeze
Blowing over the meadows brown.

And one was safe and asleep in his bed
Who at the bridge would be first to fall,
Who that day would be lying dead,
Pierced by a British musket-ball.

You know the rest. In the books you have read,
How the British Regulars fired and fled –
How the farmers gave them ball for ball,
From behind each fence and farm-yard wall,
Chasing the red-coats down the lane,
Then crossing the fields to emerge again
Under the trees at the turn of the road,
And only pausing to fire and load.

So through the night rode Paul Revere;
And so through the night went his cry of alarm
To every Middlesex village and farm –
A cry of defiance and not of fear,
A voice in the darkness, a knock at the door,
And a word that shall echo forevermore!
For, borne on the night-wind of the Past,
Through all our history, to the last,
In the hour of darkness and peril and need,
The people will waken and listen to hear
The hurrying hoof-beats of that steed,
And the midnight message of Paul Revere.

**I Heard the Bells on Christmas Day
by Henry Wadsworth Longfellow**

I heard the bells on Christmas Day

Their old, familiar carols play,
and wild and sweet
The words repeat
Of peace on earth, good-will to men!

And thought how, as the day had come,
The belfries of all Christendom
Had rolled along
The unbroken song
Of peace on earth, good-will to men!

Till ringing, singing on its way,
The world revolved from night to day,
A voice, a chime,
A chant sublime
Of peace on earth, good-will to men!

Then from each black, accursed mouth
The cannon thundered in the South,
And with the sound
The carols drowned
Of peace on earth, good-will to men!

It was as if an earthquake rent
The hearth-stones of a continent,
And made forlorn
The households born
Of peace on earth, good-will to men!

And in despair I bowed my head;
"There is no peace on earth," I said;

"For hate is strong,
And mocks the song
Of peace on earth, good-will to men!"

Then pealed the bells more loud and deep:
"God is not dead, nor doth He sleep;
The Wrong shall fail,
The Right prevail,
With peace on earth, good-will to men."

**The Concord Bridge
by Ralph Waldo Emerson**

By the rude bridge that arched the flood,
Their flag to April's breeze unfurled,
Here once the embattled farmers stood,
And fired the shot heard round the world.

The foe long since in silence slept;
Alike the conqueror silent sleeps;
And Time the ruined bridge has swept
Down the dark stream which seaward creeps.

On this green bank, by this soft stream,
We set to-day a votive stone;
That memory may their deed redeem,
When, like our sires, our sons are gone.

Spirit, that made those heroes dare,
To die, and leave their children free,
Bid Time and Nature gently spare

The shaft we raise to them and thee.

Carpe Diem
by Robert Frost

Age saw two quiet children
Go loving by at twilight,
He knew not whether homeward,
Or outward from the village,
Or (chimes were ringing) churchward,
He waited, (they were strangers)
Till they were out of hearing
To bid them both be happy.
'Be happy, happy, happy,
And seize the day of pleasure.'
The age-long theme is Age's.
'Twas Age imposed on poems
Their gather-roses burden
To warn against the danger
That overtaken lovers
From being overflooded
With happiness should have it.
And yet not know they have it.
But bid life seize the present?
It lives less in the present
Than in the future always,
And less in both together
Than in the past. The present
Is too much for the senses,
Too crowding, too confusing–
Too present to imagine.

Democracy
by Langston Hughes

Democracy will not come
Today, this year
Nor ever
Through compromise and fear.

I have as much right
As the other fellow has
To stand
On my two feet
And own the land.

I tire so of hearing people say,
Let things take their course.
Tomorrow is another day.
I do not need my freedom when I'm dead.
I cannot live on tomorrow's bread.

Freedom
Is a strong seed
Planted
In a great need.

I live here, too.
I want freedom
Just as you.

O Captain! My Captain!
by Walt Whitman

O Captain! my Captain! our fearful trip is done,
The ship has weather'd every rack, the prize we sought is won,
The port is near, the bells I hear, the people all exulting,
While follow eyes the steady keel, the vessel grim and daring;
But O heart! heart! heart!
O the bleeding drops of red,
Where on the deck my Captain lies,
Fallen cold and dead.

O Captain! my Captain! rise up and hear the bells;
Rise up–for you the flag is flung–for you the bugle trills,
For you bouquets and ribbon'd wreaths–for you the shores a-crowding,
For you they call, the swaying mass, their eager faces turning;
Here Captain! dear father!
This arm beneath your head!
It is some dream that on the deck,
You've fallen cold and dead.

My Captain does not answer, his lips are pale and still,
My father does not feel my arm, he has no pulse nor will,
The ship is anchor'd safe and sound, its voyage closed and done,
From fearful trip the victor ship comes in with object won;
Exult O shores, and ring O bells!

But I with mournful tread,
Walk the deck my Captain lies,
Fallen cold and dead.

Our Mother Pocahontas
by Vachel Lindsay
from 'For America at War'
Pocahontas' body, lovely at a poplar, sweet as a red haw in November or a pawpaw in May–did she wonder? does she remember–in the dust–in the cool tombs? **Carl Sandburg**

I

POWHATAN was conqueror,
Powhatan was emperor.
He was akin to wolf and bee,
Brother of the hickory tree;
Son of the red lightning stroke
And the lightning-shivered oak.
His panther-grace bloomed in the maid
Who laughed among the winds, and played
In excellence of savage pride,
Wooing the forest, open-eyed,
In the springtime,
In Virginia,
Our mother, Pocahontas.
Her skin was rosy copper-red,
And high she held her beauteous head.
Her step was like a rustling leaf,
Her heart a nest untouched of grief.
She dreamed of sons like Powhatan,

And through her blood the lightning ran.
Love-cries with the birds she sung,
And bird-like in the ivy swung.
The Forest, arching low and wide
Gloried in its Indian bride.
Rolfe, that dim adventurer,
Had not come a courtier.
John Rolfe is not our ancestor–
We rise from out the soul of her
Held in native wonderland
While the sun's rays kissed her hand,
In the springtime,
In Virginia,
Our mother, Pocahontas.

II

She heard the forest talking,
Across the sea came walking,
And traced the paths of Daniel Boone,
Then westward chased the painted moon.
She passed with wild young feet
On to Kansas wheat,
On to the miners' west,
The echoing cañon's guest;
Then the Pacific sand,
Waking,
Thrilling,
The midnight land …

On Adams street and Jefferson–

Flames coming up from the ground!
On Jackson street and Washington—
Flames coming up from the ground!
And why, until the dawning sun
Are flames coming up from the ground?
Because, through drowsy Springfield sped
This red-skin queen, with feathered head,
With winds and stars that pay her court,
And leaping beasts that make her sport;
Because gray Europe's rags august
She tramples in the dust;
Because we are her fields of corn;
Because our fires are all reborn
From her bosom's deathless embers,
Flaming as she remembers
The springtime
And Virginia,
Our mother, Pocahontas.

III

We here renounce our Saxon blood.
Tomorrow's hopes, an April flood,
Come roaring in. The newest race
Is born of her resilient grace.
We here renounce our Teuton pride,
Our Norse and Slavic boasts have died,
Italian dreams are swept away,
And Celtic feuds are lost today ...

She sings of lilacs, maples, wheat;

Her own soil sings beneath her feet,
Of springtime
And Virginia,
Our mother, Pocahontas.

The Little Boy and the Old Man
by Shel Silverstein

Said the little boy, "Sometimes I drop my spoon."
Said the old man, "I do that too."
The little boy whispered, "I wet my pants."
"I do that too," laughed the little old man.
Said the little boy, "I often cry."
The old man nodded, "So do I."
"But worst of all," said the boy, "it seems
Grown-ups don't pay attention to me."
And he felt the warmth of a wrinkled old hand.
"I know what you mean," said the little old man.

The Road Not Taken
by Robert Frost

Two roads diverged in a yellow wood,
And sorry I could not travel both
And be one traveler, long I stood
And looked down one as far as I could
To where it bent in the undergrowth;

Then took the other, as just as fair,
And having perhaps the better claim,
Because it was grassy and wanted wear;

Though as for that the passing there
Had worn them really about the same,

And both that morning equally lay
In leaves no step had trodden black.
Oh, I kept the first for another day!
Yet knowing how way leads on to way,
I doubted if I should ever come back.

I shall be telling this with a sigh
Somewhere ages and ages hence:
Two roads diverged in a wood, and I–
I took the one less traveled by,
And that has made all the difference.

Account of A Visit From St. Nicholas ('Twas the Night Before Christmas)
by Ralph Waldo Emerson and Clement Clarke Moore (both are attributed with authoring this poem that is a favorite by many)

'Twas the night before Christmas, when all thro' the house,
Not a creature was stirring, not even a mouse;

The stockings were hung by the chimney with care,
In hopes that St. Nicholas soon would be there;

The children were nestled all snug in their beds,
While visions of sugar plums danc'd in their heads,

And Mama in her 'kerchief, and I in my cap,
Had just settled our brains for a long winter's nap–

When out on the lawn there arose such a clatter,
I sprang from the bed to see what was the matter.

Away to the window I flew like a flash,
Tore open the shutters, and threw up the sash.

The moon on the breast of the new fallen snow,
Gave the lustre of mid-day to objects below;

When, what to my wondering eyes should appear,
But a miniature sleigh, and eight tiny reindeer,

With a little old driver, so lively and quick,
I knew in a moment it must be St. Nick.

More rapid than eagles his coursers they came,
And he whistled, and shouted, and call'd them by name:

"Now! Dasher, now! Dancer, now! Prancer, and Vixen,
"On! Comet, on! Cupid, on! Dunder and Blixem!;

To the top of the porch! to the top of the wall!
Now dash away! dash away! dash away all!"

As dry leaves before the wild hurricane fly,
When they meet with an obstacle, mount to the sky;

So up to the house-top the coursers they flew,

With the sleigh full of Toys – and St. Nicholas too:

And then in a twinkling, I heard on the roof
The prancing and pawing of each little hoof.

As I drew in my head, and was turning around,
Down the chimney St. Nicholas came with a bound:

He was dress'd all in fur, from his head to his foot,
And his clothes were all tarnish'd with ashes and soot;

A bundle of toys was flung on his back,
And he look'd like a peddler just opening his pack:

His eyes—how they twinkled! his dimples how merry,
His cheeks were like roses, his nose like a cherry;

His droll little mouth was drawn up like a bow.
And the beard of his chin was as white as the snow;

The stump of a pipe he held tight in his teeth,
And the smoke it encircled his head like a wreath.

He had a broad face, and a little round belly
That shook when he laugh'd, like a bowl full of jelly:

He was chubby and plump, a right jolly old elf,
And I laugh'd when I saw him in spite of myself;

A wink of his eye and a twist of his head
Soon gave me to know I had nothing to dread.

He spoke not a word, but went straight to his work,
And fill'd all the stockings; then turn'd with a jerk,

And laying his finger aside of his nose
And giving a nod, up the chimney he rose.

He sprung to his sleigh, to his team gave a whistle,
And away they all flew, like the down of a thistle:

But I heard him exclaim, ere he drove out of sight–
Happy Christmas to all, and to all a good night.

Casey at the Bat
by Ernest Lawrence Thayer
A Ballad of the Republic, Sung in the Year 1888

The outlook wasn't brilliant for the Mudville nine that day;
The score stood four to two with but one inning more to play.
And then when Cooney died at first, and Barrows did the same,
A sickly silence fell upon the patrons of the game.

A straggling few got up to go in deep despair. The rest
Clung to that hope which springs eternal in the human breast;
They thought if only Casey could but get a whack at that–
We'd put up even money now with Casey at the bat.

But Flynn preceded Casey, as did also Jimmy Blake,
And the former was a lulu and the latter was a cake;
So upon that stricken multitude grim melancholy sat,
For there seemed but little chance of Casey's getting to the bat.

But Flynn let drive a single, to the wonderment of all,
And Blake, the much despised, tore the cover off the ball;
And when the dust had lifted, and men saw what had occurred,
There was Jimmy safe at second and Flynn a-hugging third.

Then from 5,000 throats and more there rose a lusty yell;
It rumbled through the valley, it rattled in the dell;
It knocked upon the mountain and recoiled upon the flat,
For Casey, mighty Casey, was advancing to the bat.

There was ease in Casey's manner as he stepped into his place;
There was pride in Casey's bearing and a smile on Casey's face.
And when, responding to the cheers, he lightly doffed his hat,
No stranger in the crowd could doubt 'twas Casey at the bat.

Ten thousand eyes were on him as he rubbed his hands with dirt;
Five thousand tongues applauded when he wiped them on his shirt.

Then while the writhing pitcher ground the ball into his hip,
Defiance gleamed in Casey's eye, a sneer curled Casey's lip.

And now the leather-covered sphere came hurtling through the air,
And Casey stood a-watching it in haughty grandeur there.
Close by the sturdy batsman the ball unheeded sped–
"That ain't my style," said Casey. "Strike one," the umpire said.

From the benches, black with people, there went up a muffled roar,
Like the beating of the storm-waves on a stern and distant shore.
"Kill him! Kill the umpire!" shouted someone on the stand;
And it's likely they'd have killed him had not Casey raised his hand.

With a smile of Christian charity great Casey's visage shone;
He stilled the rising tumult; he bade the game go on;
He signaled to the pitcher, and once more the spheroid flew;
But Casey still ignored it, and the umpire said, "Strike two."

"Fraud!" cried the maddened thousands, and echo answered fraud;

But one scornful look from Casey and the audience was awed.
They saw his face grow stern and cold, they saw his muscles strain,
And they knew that Casey wouldn't let that ball go by again.

The sneer is gone from Casey's lip, his teeth are clinched in hate;
He pounds with cruel violence his bat upon the plate.
And now the pitcher holds the ball, and now he lets it go,
And now the air is shattered by the force of Casey's blow.

Oh, somewhere in this favored land the sun is shining bright;
The band is playing somewhere, and somewhere hearts are light,
And somewhere men are laughing, and somewhere children shout;
But there is no joy in Mudville—mighty Casey has struck out.

Drum-Taps
by Walt Whitman

Aroused and angry,
I thought to beat the alarum, and urge relentless war;
But soon my fingers fail'd me, my face droop'd, and I resign'd
myself,

To sit by the wounded and soothe them, or silently watch
the dead.

FIRST, O songs, for a prelude,
Lightly strike on the stretch'd tympanum, pride and joy in
my city,
How she led the rest to arms – how she gave the cue,
How at once with lithe limbs, unwaiting a moment, she
sprang;
(O superb! O Manhattan, my own, my peerless!
O strongest you in the hour of danger, in crisis! O truer
than steel!)
How you sprang! how you threw off the costumes of
peace with
indifferent hand;
How your soft opera-music changed, and the drum and
fife were heard
in their stead;
How you led to the war, (that shall serve for our prelude,
songs of
soldiers,)
How Manhattan drum-taps led.

Forty years had I in my city seen soldiers parading;
Forty years as a pageant – till unawares, the Lady of this
teeming and
turbulent city,
Sleepless amid her ships, her houses, her incalculable
wealth,
With her million children around her – suddenly,
At dead of night, at news from the south,

Incens'd, struck with clench'd hand the pavement.

A shock electric – the night sustain'd it;
Till with ominous hum, our hive at day-break pour'd out
its myriads.

From the houses then, and the workshops, and through all
the
doorways,
Leapt they tumultuous – and lo! Manhattan arming.

To the drum-taps prompt,
The young men falling in and arming;
The mechanics arming, (the trowel, the jack-plane, the
blacksmith's
hammer, tost aside with precipitation;)
The lawyer leaving his office, and arming – the judge
leaving the
court;
The driver deserting his wagon in the street, jumping
down, throwing
the reins abruptly down on the horses' backs;
The salesman leaving the store – the boss, book-keeper,
porter, all
leaving;
Squads gather everywhere by common consent, and arm;
The new recruits, even boys – the old men show them how
to wear their
Accoutrements – they buckle the straps carefully;
Outdoors arming – indoors arming – the flash of the
musket-barrels;

The white tents cluster in camps – the arm'd sentries around – the
sunrise cannon, and again at sunset;
Arm'd regiments arrive every day, pass through the city, and embark
from the wharves;
(How good they look, as they tramp down to the river, sweaty, with
their guns on their shoulders!
How I love them! how I could hug them, with their brown faces, and
their clothes and knapsacks cover'd with dust!)
The blood of the city up – arm'd! arm'd! the cry everywhere;
The flags flung out from the steeples of churches, and from all the
public buildings and stores;
The tearful parting – the mother kisses her son – the son kisses his
mother;
(Loth is the mother to part – yet not a word does she speak to detain
him;)
The tumultuous escort – the ranks of policemen preceding, clearing the
way;
The unpent enthusiasm – the wild cheers of the crowd for their
favorites;
The artillery – the silent cannons, bright as gold, drawn along,

rumble lightly over the stones; 40
(Silent cannons – soon to cease your silence!
Soon, unlimber'd, to begin the red business;)
All the mutter of preparation – all the determin'd arming;
The hospital service – the lint, bandages, and medicines;
The women volunteering for nurses – the work begun for, in earnest – no
mere parade now;
War! an arm'd race is advancing! – the welcome for battle – no turning
away;
War! be it weeks, months, or years – an arm'd race is advancing to
welcome it.

Mannahatta a-march! – and it's O to sing it well!
It's O for a manly life in the camp!
And the sturdy artillery! 50
The guns, bright as gold – the work for giants – to serve well the
guns:
Unlimber them! no more, as the past forty years, for salutes for
courtesies merely;
Put in something else now besides powder and wadding.

And you, Lady of Ships! you Mannahatta!
Old matron of this proud, friendly, turbulent city!
Often in peace and wealth you were pensive, or covertly frown'd amid
all your children;

But now you smile with joy, exulting old Mannahatta!

www.ingramcontent.com/pod-product-compliance
Lightning Source LLC
LaVergne TN
LVHW041647060526
838200LV00040B/1755